The Magical Red Kimono

May you always find the magic!

— Lyn Morrill

The Magical Red Kimono
Copyright 2025 - Jan Morrill
Artwork Copyright 2025 - Jan Morrill
All Rights Reserved

No part of this book may be reproduced or transmitted in any form or by any means, electronic or mechanical, including photocopying, recording, or by any information storage and retrieval system, without permission in writing from the author.

Library of Congress Number: 2025905944

All photos courtesy of Densho
Jan Morrill - Illustrator
Clarissa Willis - Publishing Coordinator
Sharon Kizziah-Holmes - Book Design

SOLANDER PRESS
Springdale, Arkansas

ISBN: 978-1-966675-06-8 (Paperback)
ISBN: 978-1-966675-07-5 (Hardback)
ISBN: 978-1-966675-08-2 (eBook)

Dedication

To my grandchildren with love:
Tommy
Allie
Jack
Harry
Penelope
May your friendships open your hearts to the world.

The Magical Red Kimono

Written and
Illustrated By
Jan Morrill

Rohwer Relocation Center
Arkansas

One summer day in Arkansas, Sachi and her best friend, Jubie, sat in the shade of a big oak tree that grew outside the internment camp known as Rohwer. Together, they listened to the wind whispering through the leaves.

Jubie wiped her face with her bandana. "I'm hot," she said.

"Me, too," Sachi replied, as she stared at the parade of clouds drifting by.

Suddenly, she pointed at one. "Hey! That looks like a kimono!"

Jubie crinkled her nose, the way she often did before asking a question. "What's a kimono?"

"It's a Japanese dress," said Sachi. "Like the one I wear when I dance at Obon."

"O-what?" Jubie asked.

Sachi and Jubie were quiet again as they stared at the sky. The kimono cloud began to look like a dinosaur.

Sachi yawned. "I'm bored," she said.

Jubie nodded. "Me, too. We need an adventure!"

Then, Sachi thought of something and jumped up with excitement. "I know what we can do!" she said. "I'll teach you a Japanese dance! You can even wear my kimono. I just need to run back to the barracks to get it!"

Jubie clapped her hands. "Oh boy! That sounds like fun!"

"Hey!" Jubie said. "Is your dance anything like the Boogie Woogie? I'm real good at that one."

Sachi covered her mouth with her hands so Jubie wouldn't see her giggle. "No, it's not like the Boogie Woogie. Wait here. I'll be right back with my kimono," she said.

As Sachi walked through the camp gate, she thought of something else and called across the road to Jubie. "If you learn the dance, maybe you can come to Obon with me!"

When Sachi returned with her kimono, Jubie's eyes widened as she traced the flowers with her finger. "It's beautiful," she whispered.

"Put it on! I'll help you with the obi," said Sachi.

"Obi?" Jubie asked, rolling her eyes. "I thought you said it was called Obon."

Sachi laughed. "I know it's confusing. Obon is the dance festival. Obi is the belt that is tied around the kimono," she said as she tightened the obi around Jubie's waist.

"Oh, I get it now." Jubie stretched her arms and waved them in the air. "The sleeves are so pretty. I feel like a butterfly!"

Jubie started to dance the Boogie Woogie. But when she twirled around, she almost tripped. "Oops! Guess I best not Boogie Woogie in a kimono," Jubie said. "How do I look?"

"So pretty," Sachi replied. How bright the kimono's colors looked against Jubie's skin. "Now, are you ready to learn Bon-Odori?" she asked.

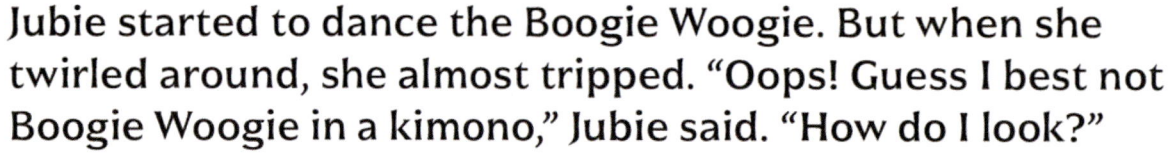

Jubie huffed. "Learn what? I thought you said I was going to learn Obon."

Sachi shook her head. "You're going to learn the dance called Bon-Odori so you can go to the festival called Obon." She started to hum and dance.

"What are you humming?" asked Jubie.

"It's called 'Tankō Bushi'," Sachi replied. "It means 'Song of Coal Miners' in English."

Jubie snickered. "Sure doesn't sound like a coal miner's song to me."

"It's an old folk song about a coal mine in Japan," Sachi said. "That's where my mama was born. Just remember. It's a song about coal miners. It'll help you learn the steps."

"First clap your hands three times. Then, pretend you're holding a shovel," Sachi said, as she showed Jubie the moves. "Next, act like you're scooping coal. Scoop twice to the right, then twice to the left."

"Next, make-believe your hands are butterflies," Sachi said, showing Jubie. "And make believe the butterflies are flying to the moon. Last, clap three times. Then, just do it all over again."

As Sachi watched Jubie dance, she thought the kimono must be magic. How else could Jubie—who wasn't Japanese—move as if she'd danced the Bon-Odori a hundred times before? With each graceful step, the long, silken sleeves floated like kites in the summer breeze.

How beautiful Jubie looked. Until . . .

There it was! That funny way Jubie held her mouth every time she was concentrating hard on something.

Sachi laughed out loud.

"Are you laughing at me?" Jubie asked. "Because if you are, just wait until I teach you the Boogie Woogie. Now that'll be funny! But for now, will you please untie this obi so I can breathe?"

As Sachi untied the obi, she said, "Today, you learned the difference between obi, Bon-Odori and Obon! And your dance was so pretty, I think my red kimono might just be magic! I can't wait until everyone sees you dance."

Once the obi was loosened, Jubie grabbed her tummy and laughed out loud. "I can't wait to teach you my dance. You'll love the Boogie Woogie!"

AUTHOR'S NOTE

The Magical Red Kimono is based on a scene from my historical fiction, The Red Kimono. (University of Arkansas Press, 2013)

After the attack on Pearl Harbor, questions and fears about the loyalty of people of Japanese descent began to arise. President Franklin D. Roosevelt's Executive Order 9066 ordered approximately 120,000 people of Japanese descent to be interned in ten relocation centers located around the United States. Two thirds of the internees were American citizens. Many were children.

Approximately 16,000 internees were brought from the west coast by train to two different camps in Arkansas: Rohwer and Jerome.

Nine of the ten relocation camps were closed by the end of 1945, with the exception of Tule Lake, which closed in 1946. Most internees returned to California. However, some relocated to other states. Some returned to Japan.

SUGGESTED READING AND RESOURCES

Non-Fiction
Inada, Lawon Fusao, ed. *Only What We Could Carry: The Japanese American Internment Experience.* Berkeley: Heyday Books, 2000.
Rohwer Outpost (Rohwer Internment Camp, Arkansas). 1942–1945.
Takei, George. *To the Stars: The Autobiography of George Takei, Star Trek's Mr. Sulu.* New York: Simon and Schuster, 1994.
Tunnel, Michael O., and George W. Chilcoat. *The Children of Topaz: The Story of a Japanese-American Internment Camp.* New York: Holiday House, 1996.
Uchida, Yoshiko. *Desert Exile: The Uprooting of a Japanese-American Family.* Seattle: University of Washington Press, 1982.

Fiction
Dallas, Sandra. *Tallgrass.* New York: St. Martin's Press, 2007.
Ford, Jamie. *Hotel on the Corner of Bitter and Sweet.* New York: Ballantine Books, 2009.
Guterson, David. *Snow Falling on Cedars.* New York: Harcourt Brace & Company, 1994.
Houston, Jeanne Wakatsuki, and James D. Houston. *Farewell to Manzanar.* Boston: Houghton Mifflin Company, 1973.
Schiffer, Vivienne. *Camp Nine,* Fayetteville: The University of Arkansas Press, 2011.

Video
Kintsukuroi, directed by Kerwin Berk (Ikeibi Films, 2025), DVD.
Time of Fear, directed by Sue Williams. Perf. George Takei. (PBS Home Video, 2005), DVD.

Websites
Densho: The Japanese American Legacy Project, www.densho.org.
Heart Mountain Wyoming Foundation, www.heartmountain.org.
Jerome Rohwer Committee, https://jeromerohwer.org.
Rohwer Japanese American Relocation Center Museum, https://rohwer.astate.edu/
The Japanese American National Museum, www.janm.org.
Tule Lake Committee, https://www.tulelake.org.

All photos courtesy of Densho.org

JAN MORRILL was born and (mostly) raised in California. Her mother, a Buddhist Japanese American, was an internee during World War II. Her father, a Southern Baptist redhead of Irish descent, retired from the Air Force. Many of her stories reflect memories of growing up in a multicultural, multi-religious, multi-political environment. An artist as well as a writer, Jan is currently working on the sequel to her historical fiction, *The Red Kimono*. (University of Arkansas Press, 2013)

Visit her at www.janmorrill.com.

www.ingramcontent.com/pod-product-compliance
Lightning Source LLC
LaVergne TN
LVRC090827240525
811697LV00009B/55